Jasper John Dooley
Star of the Week

Jasper John Dooley
Star of the Week

Written by Caroline Adderson
Illustrated by Ben Clanton

Kids Can Press

For Sophie Anastasia Elizabeth Campbell,
a little watermelon — C.A.

First paperback edition 2014

Kids Can Press acknowledges the financial support of the Government of Ontario, through the Ontario Media Development Corporation's Ontario Book Initiative; the Ontario Arts Council; the Canada Council for the Arts; and the Government of Canada, through the CBF, for our publishing activity.

Published in Canada by
Kids Can Press Ltd.
25 Dockside Drive
Toronto, ON M5A 0B5

Published in the U.S. by
Kids Can Press Ltd
2250 Military Road
Tonawanda, NY 14150

www.kidscanpress.com

Edited by Sheila Barry
Designed by Rachel Di Salle

The hardcover edition of this book is smyth sewn casebound.
The paperback edition of this book is limp sewn with a drawn-on cover.
Manufactured in Shen Zhen, Guang Dong, P.R. China, in 10/2013 by Printplus Limited

CM 12 0 9 8 7 6 5 4 3 2
CM PA 14 0 9 8 7 6 5 4 3 2 1

Library and Archives Canada Cataloguing in Publication

Adderson, Caroline, 1963–
     Jasper John Dooley star of the week / written by Caroline Adderson ; illustrated by Ben Clanton.

(Jasper John Dooley ; 1)
For ages 7–10.
ISBN 978-1-55453-578-1 (bound) ISBN 978-1-77138-119-2 (pbk.)

I. Clanton, Ben, 1988– II. Title. III. Series: Adderson, Caroline, 1963– Jasper John Dooley ; 1

PS8551.D3267J38 2012   jC813'.54   C2011-904726-8

Kids Can Press is a **Corus**™ Entertainment company

Contents

Chapter 1

Jasper John Dooley was in the basement getting ready for a busy week. The kid who was the Star of the Week was always busy and, starting tomorrow, Jasper was the Star. Jasper, the Star! Tomorrow! He'd looked forward to tomorrow for a very, very, very long time.

Mom came down with a load of rumpled clothes in her arms. "Yay!" Jasper said. "Laundry!"

"Aah!" she said. "Jasper John, you scared me! What are you doing down here? Why aren't you playing outside?"

"I'm the Star of the Week," he said.

"You're the Star of the Week tomorrow," Mom said, opening the lid of the washing machine. "Today you're a boy who needs to breathe fresh air."

The door of the washing machine looked like a big square mouth. Mom began stuffing the clothes down into it, feeding it dirty socks and T-shirts and soggy towels. "Did you see the schedule?" Jasper asked her.

"It's in the kitchen."

"On Monday, the Star gets to do Show and Tell," Jasper said. "Only the Star gets to do Show and Tell. I'll Show and I'll Tell. Everybody else will Look and Listen."

"Still," Mom said, "it's such a beautiful day. Here you are hiding in the basement."

"I'm not hiding. I'm collecting the lint off the dryer screen."

Jasper had already pulled the screen out of its slot and scraped off the lint. Now the lint sat on top of the dryer, a flowery-smelling, gray, linty blob. "It's my Show and Tell," Jasper said. Then, in case Mom hadn't read the schedule very closely, in case she had just magnetted it to the fridge with the store coupons and emergency phone numbers and the long list of Things To Do that never got crossed off, only longer, Jasper reminded her what was going to happen that week at school.

"Monday, Show and Tell. Tuesday, Family Tree. Wednesday, Science Experiment. Thursday, I Share My Talent. And on Friday …"

He stopped so he could enjoy a shiver of excitement.

"On Friday, I bring a Special Snack for everybody to eat while they're writing Compliments to me."

"It's going to be a wonderful week, Jasper," Mom said as she poured the detergent into the hungry mouth of the washing machine. Jasper watched her. "Detergent is ketchup to a washing machine," he said, but she wasn't listening. She said, "You have your lint, Jasper. Now go outside."

"When's the laundry going to be finished?" he asked.

"In a few hours. Why?"

"I need more lint."

"Oh, Jasper," Mom said, and she pointed to the basement door.

Jasper went upstairs to get his lint box from his room. Out in the backyard, he sat with his legs in a *V* in the grass and carefully opened the box. He stuck his nose in it and sniffed that special flowery lint smell, the fabric softener clean-clothes-start-of-a-new-day smell that he loved.

His Nan had given him the box. It was red with a gold latch and compartments inside for bracelets and earrings and rings. But Jasper wasn't using it for jewelry. He was filling each of the compartments with lint. He packed the new blob in one of the gray-lint compartments. Lint with colored flecks went in a different compartment. There was also a compartment for pocket lint and a very, very special compartment that had only a tiny bit of lint in it because that kind of lint was rare and hard to collect. It was belly-button lint, and the only place Jasper could get belly-button lint was in his dad's belly button.

After he had sorted his lint, he took the box inside and told his mom he was going across the alley and one house down to see what his friend Ori was doing. "Good," she said. "Play outside."

A sound like the wa-wa-wa of a car alarm floated across Ori's yard. Ori lived with his mother and father, just like Jasper. Except Ori's mom was expecting a baby and for a month now had been going around looking like there was a watermelon stuffed under her shirt. Once, when Jasper mentioned it to Ori, Ori said, "Maybe it is! Maybe it is a watermelon!" Since then, whenever they talked about the baby, which wasn't very often, they called it the watermelon. Jasper rang the doorbell, but nobody answered because of wa-wa-wa-wa coming from the open kitchen window. A watermelon or a baby? Jasper wondered. He was pretty sure he knew which one it was.

He knocked loudly. Finally, Ori came to the door wearing a winter hat with earflaps. The strings that held the flaps down were tied in a bow under his chin.

"Hi," Ori said.

"Hi," Jasper said.

"What?" Ori said, cupping an earflap.

Jasper asked, "Is that the Watermelon crying?"

Ori stepped outside and closed the door behind him. "What did you say? I couldn't hear you."

"Did the Watermelon come?" Jasper asked.

"Unfortunately."

"When?"

"Friday, but they only brought it home today."

"Can I see it?"

"Are you sure you want to?" Ori asked.

When Jasper said he did, Ori made a face. He motioned for Jasper to cover his ears. The boys went inside pressing their hands to the sides of their heads. Ori pressed his earflaps.

"Is it a girl watermelon or a boy watermelon?" Jasper asked, but Ori didn't hear him.

In the living room, Ori's dad was walking around in a circle. All his walking had flattened a path in the living room carpet. He rounded the circle with his arms full of crying, which was when Jasper saw that Ori's dad had orange things sticking out of both ears. They looked like baby carrots but turned out to be earplugs.

"Jasper!" Ori's dad said. "Look at Ori's new sister!"

He stopped and held the baby out.

Jasper came over. Purple! A purple baby! Somehow he had expected her to be red, like the inside of a watermelon.

"Isn't she beautiful?!" Ori's dad yelled.

"Yes," Jasper said. He liked her little purple face and the way her tongue pushed back in her mouth and quivered. "She doesn't have any teeth," Jasper said, but nobody heard him.

"Come on," Ori said, tugging Jasper by the arm. "Let's get out of here."

"I like her!" Jasper told Ori as they went back down the hall. "She's purple!"

"The thing is," Ori said, "all she does is cry."

Just then, Ori's mother came out of the bedroom wearing orange earplugs, too, and a really tired face. She smiled at Jasper. She patted Ori's hat. And she still looked like she was carrying a watermelon!

Jasper and Ori went outside. "Did you remember I'm the Star of the Week tomorrow?" Jasper asked.

"No."

“Well, I am,” Jasper said. What a good Show and Tell a baby would be, he thought, and suddenly he felt very, very glad that Ori had already been the Star of the Week and brought a model airplane for Show and Tell.

☆ ☆ ☆

The rest of the day Jasper couldn’t stop thinking about Ori’s baby sister and her little wrinkled purple face. He wondered how he could ever have imagined she was a watermelon. A watermelon! She was the opposite of a watermelon — small and purple. She was a plum!

At supper that night, he announced that he wanted a baby, too. “A purple one,” he said. “The purple ones are the nicest.”

"Nicer than the green ones?" Dad asked.

"There's no such thing as a green baby."

"Where would we get a purple baby?" Mom asked.

"You grow it in your stomach and then you go to the hospital and have it taken out," Jasper told her. "Everybody knows that."

Mom patted her stomach. "But I don't have anything growing in here right now."

"I bet they have extras at the hospital," Jasper said.

Dad told Jasper, "I remember when you were born. I got to hold you for a minute before the nurse whisked you off. I used to think that all babies were the same. But when I looked for you later in the nursery, I knew which one you were right away."

Jasper had heard this story before. "I was the one with lots and lots of black hair sticking out all over my head. Why didn't you call me Licorice?"

"Licorice?" they said.

"When we get a baby, I'm going to name her Plum," Jasper said.

"Who wants dessert?" Mom asked, getting up from the table. She seemed to be changing the subject.

"I do!" Dad and Jasper called.

"But it's just too bad!" Jasper said when Mom came back with the ice cream and three bowls.

"What?" she asked. "What's too bad?"

"That we don't have Plum right now. If we did, I could bring her for Show and Tell tomorrow. That would be the best Show and Tell anybody ever saw."

"I don't know about that," Dad said. "Yours is pretty good, too. Some of those kids won't ever have seen belly-button lint before."

Chapter 2

The next morning, Jasper got out of bed the second he woke up. Usually, he fell back to sleep a few more times to watch the end of his dream, but today he didn't want to get the lates. Today he was the Star of the Week.

He went to the kitchen and stared at the hands on the oven clock. Seven five, ten, fifteen, twenty. Seven twenty-five. There was lots of time not to get the lates. He went to Mom and Dad's room and, standing by their bed, spread his arms wide. "Presenting — the Star of the Week!"

Mom sat up clutching the covers around her neck. "Ah! Jasper John!"

"It's just me," he told her. "The Star of the Week."

Dad opened one eye at the clock radio on the bedside table. "It's five-thirty," he said.

"Oops," Jasper said. "I got the hands wrong. Again."

Dad rolled over and covered his head with his pillow. "Go back to bed, Jasper," Mom said.

"I don't want to get the lates," Jasper said.

"Just go," Mom said, making shooing motions with her hands. "We'll make sure you don't get the lates."

"I'm always getting the lates."

"Go!"

"Okay," Jasper said, backing out of the room, "but don't forget — I'm the Star!"

Jasper went back to his bed. He tried to fall asleep again, but he was too excited. Why not just go? Just go to school right now? So he got out of bed and ran the block to school. A big banner covered the front of the building. JASPER JOHN DOOLEY, STAR OF THE WEEK! All the kids in the school, not just the kids from Jasper's class, all the kids were leaning out the windows waving little flags and chanting, "Jasper! Jasper! Jasper!" Jasper ran up the steps. He pulled and pulled on the door handle, but it wouldn't open. Now all the kids were chanting, "Late! Late! Late!" Then Mom woke Jasper, which was a good thing because in the dream he was still wearing his pajamas.

Chapter 3

Ms. Tosh took the star out of the top drawer of her desk. It was a fabric star with gold sparkles glued all over it. She safety-pinned it onto Jasper's chest. "It's yours to wear for the day," she said.

"Even lunch and recess?" the Star asked.

"Yes. But when the bell rings at the end of the day, give it back. It will be safer here in my drawer."

The first special thing the Star got to do was the calendar. When Ms. Tosh asked the month, the day of the week and the date, anybody could put up his hand to answer. But only the Star got to slide the right cards into the slots on the calendar. Jasper enjoyed this, but what he was really looking forward to was Show and Tell, which came next.

Jasper carried his box to the front of the classroom. All the kids leaned over their tables, curious about what Jasper had brought. Jasper smiled. He pushed his chest out so the star would show better and turned to Ms. Tosh, so she could introduce him.

Then the door to the classroom opened, and Ori slipped inside. He looked really tired. He looked like nobody had made him wash his face. "Hurry, hurry, Ori," Ms. Tosh told him, which sent him scurrying over to the table he shared with Leon and Isabel. "We're about to start."

Jasper was surprised that Ori was late. Ori lived across the alley and one house down from Jasper. Jasper lived the closest to the school, and Ori the second closest. Ori never got the lates the way Jasper did. Jasper got the lates about twice a week, even though he lived just one block away. But not today. Today Jasper was the Star, and the Star had arrived in plenty of time with his box of lint under his arm.

Now the Star of the Week stood at the front of the room with Nan's old jewelry box in his hands. Once all the kids were settled again, which took a long time, Ms. Tosh said, "Our Star, Jasper, has brought us something for Show and Tell. What a wonderful box, Jasper. I wonder what's in it."

Ori's hand went up.

"What's your guess, Ori?" Ms. Tosh asked.

"I don't know," Ori said. "I just wanted to tell you that my mom brought the baby home yesterday."

"A baby! How wonderful! A girl or a boy?"

"A girl," Ori said. "The thing is, she cries all, all, all the time."

"Babies do that," Ms. Tosh said.

Jasper touched the star on his chest to make sure it hadn't fallen off. It was still there. Jasper was still the Star waiting to do Show and Tell.

"And does she have a name?" Ms. Tosh asked Ori.

"We're trying to decide," Ori said. "My dad likes Rachel. My mom likes Anna."

Jasper lifted Nan's old jewelry box and tapped it twice with his finger. That was what Ms. Tosh always did when Jasper lost focus. She would come over to his desk and tap his worksheet.

"I like Noisy," Ori said.

Jasper put up his hand. Finally, Ms. Tosh noticed him and said, "Yes, Jasper? Do you have something to say about Ori's new baby sister?"

Jasper had been about to remind Ms. Tosh that he was the Star of the Week, but now he accidentally answered her question. "I saw her yesterday. She's purple."

"That's because she's crying all the time," Ori said.

"Am I still the Star?" Jasper asked.

"Of course you are, Jasper. It's just that a new baby is so exciting. Now Ori will have to bring in a picture to add to his Family Tree. Kids, do you see what Ori did? He left a space on his Family Tree for his new sister."

Ms. Tosh went over to where Ori's Family Tree was taped to the wall. Ori had made the best tree out of all the Stars in the class so far, with pictures of his family members cut into the shape of leaves. Even though Ori lived with just his mom and dad, like Jasper, he had a lot of aunts and uncles and even more cousins. He had as many relatives as a tree has leaves, though most of them lived far away. Ms. Tosh pointed to the bottom of the tree, next to the leaf-shaped picture of Ori. Glued there was a leaf without a picture that Jasper hadn't noticed before.

"So what's in your box, Jasper?" Ms. Tosh asked.

Finally!

Jasper let the kids try to guess what was in Nan's old jewelry box. They guessed jewelry. They guessed marbles. They guessed money.

"You're never going to guess," Jasper told them.

"Nothing's in the box," Zoë guessed. "The box is empty. The box is the Show and Tell."

"Wrong," Jasper said.

"Air's in the box!" Leon guessed.

"Wrong," Jasper said. He felt wonderful saying "wrong" over and over again.

"All right, Jasper," Ms. Tosh said. "We give up. What's in the box?"

Jasper felt all shivery undoing the gold latch. Everybody in the class leaned forward over their tables again. "Are you ready?" Jasper asked.

Everybody was waiting. It was their turn to Look and Listen.

When Jasper threw open the lid, the class leaned forward even more to see what was inside. Some of the kids at the back got up from their tables and came closer to get a better look. Ms. Tosh had to step in and shoo them back. "What is it? What is it?" they were all asking.

"Lint!" Jasper announced.

"My goodness," Ms. Tosh said. "Where did you get all that lint?"

Jasper was surprised she didn't know because he knew for a fact that she had a dryer. Once, when she was leaning over him helping with his math, he had smelled that fabric softener clean-clothes-start-of-a-new-day smell coming off of her. "Did you just wash your jacket?" he had asked. When she said she had, Jasper asked her if he could look in the pockets.

"There's nothing in them," she said.

But there was. There was some nice dark-green pocket lint that she let him keep!

Now that he had Showed, he began to Tell. "I collect lint. I've been collecting it for a long time." He pointed out that there were different kinds of lint in the box, the light gray, the dark gray and the gray flecked with bright colors that he scraped off the dryer screen. There were also all different colors of pocket lint, including the dark-green lint Ms. Tosh had given him. The pocket lint looked more like worms than blobs. Finally, there was the very rare and very special belly-button lint. When he said,

"Belly-button lint," somebody, he thought it might have been Isabel, said, "Yuck!"

He explained how hard it was to collect belly-button lint, how he had to sneak into his parents' room in the morning and very carefully lift up the covers and check his dad's belly button while he was asleep. If Jasper tried to get the lint out when his dad was awake, he would cover his belly button with his hand and run away screaming, "Stop thief! Stop!"

Everybody stared at Jasper. They didn't laugh, though Jasper always laughed when he chased his dad around the house trying to steal his belly-button lint. Dad laughed, too.

"Very, very interesting, Jasper," Ms. Tosh said. She coughed a little cough and then asked the class if they had any questions for Jasper. Lots of hands went up, but nobody asked the questions Jasper expected. They asked, "Don't you have any toys?"

What kind of question was that? "Yes," Jasper said. "I have lots of toys."

"Don't you have a garbage can?"

"A garbage can?" Jasper said. "Of course. Doesn't everybody?"

"Are you really, really poor?"

"I don't think so," Jasper said. "Why?"

Nobody asked about Jasper's Show and Tell at all. Nobody asked, "Is the smell of dryer lint your favorite smell?" Or: "Don't you love how pocket lint looks like worms, but belly-button lint looks like tiny little pills?" Or: "Is dryer lint like the ghosts of all the clothes you ever wore?"

Chapter 4

At the end of the day, Jasper went up to Ms. Tosh's desk to turn in his star. When he stuck out his chest so Ms. Tosh could unpin it, he closed his eyes, too, so he wouldn't have to see her close the star up in the drawer. Show and Tell hadn't gone very well. He knew because when Ori was Star of the Week, the kids had oooed at his model airplane. When Leon was the Star, they had oooed at his fossil. But when they saw Jasper's lint collection, they had yucked.

Jasper laid his hand on the empty place on his shirt where the star had been. He was afraid to ask, but he had to. "Do I still get to be the Star tomorrow?"

Ms. Tosh didn't seem to know what he meant. "Of course, Jasper," she told him. "You're the Star for the whole week."

Jasper felt a little better after that.

Mom was waiting for him when he came out of school carrying his box. Dad walked Jasper to school before he left for work, and Mom picked him up because Mom worked at home on her computer, doing computer things. "How did it go?" she asked.

"Okay," Jasper said. "Did you go to the hospital?"

"Did I go to the hospital? What for?"

"To see if they had any extra babies," Jasper said.

Mom blinked a few times.

"I thought you might surprise me," Jasper said.

"Because I'm the Star of the Week. And because nobody understood my Show and Tell."

"Didn't they? I'm sorry to hear that." When Mom pulled him close for a hug, the Star of the Week almost dropped his box of lint.

Jasper and his mom always waited for Ori, and then the three of them walked home together. Ori was slow today, but finally he came out of the school dragging his backpack. "Ori," Mom said, "you look terrible. Are you sick?"

"I'm tired," Ori said. "Can I come over to your house, Jasper?"

Jasper said, "I have to work on my Family Tree. On Tuesday, the Star presents his family. Remember?"

"That shouldn't take too long," Mom said. "We have a small family."

"It's going to be even harder to make a good tree because of that," Jasper told her. "You should see Ori's tree. It's so big I could climb it."

Jasper turned to Ori. "Sorry, Ori. Not today."

Ori slumped a little. When they reached the alley, he trudged away dragging his backpack behind him.

As soon as Mom and Jasper got inside, Jasper started work on his tree. He took a big piece of construction paper from the craft cupboard and a pencil from the pencil jar. First, he drew two straight lines for the trunk, then he drew a branch. On the branch, he drew three leaves — one for Mom, one for Dad and one for the Star of the Week. At the end of the same branch, he drew a little twig with two leaves — one for his Nan and one for his dad's brother, Jasper's Uncle Tom, whom they usually only saw at Christmas.

Jasper opened his box of colored pencils and sharpened two of them. Brown and green shaving flowers fluttered down. He colored the trunk, the branch and the twig brown. He colored the five leaves green. "We need more people in this family," he said, frowning at his picture.

He got an idea. He erased some bark in the middle of the tree trunk and drew a hole. In the hole, he drew a mother and a father squirrel. All around the tree and along the branch he drew squirrel children and squirrel aunts and uncles and cousins and grandparents. When he was finished, he held the drawing out. It didn't even look like a Family Tree. It looked like a Family Stick overrun with squirrels.

But it gave Jasper another idea. He crumpled up the paper and went out the back door to look around for a stick. He found a good one under the hedge and stopped to scratch his back with it. Ah! That felt good!

Now he needed cardboard for a stand. He asked his mom for a box to rip up. While she was looking for one, Jasper got the photo album and found pictures of everybody. He cut leaves out of construction paper and glued everybody on their own leaf. For himself, he made a leaf in the shape of a star and covered it with tinfoil. Mom came back with something better than cardboard, a piece of Styrofoam.

"String?" asked Jasper.

She got some yarn. Jasper hole-punched the leaves and threaded them with yarn.

"What?" Mom asked after they had hung all the leaves on the stick and glued it to the Styrofoam. "What's wrong? It looks terrific."

"It's so skinny! It looks so sad!"

Then Jasper cut out a purple leaf and hung it on the Family Stick, too. "There," he said. "That's a little better now."

☆ ☆ ☆

Jasper's Family Stick stood in the middle of the table during supper. Dad said, "I like this new decoration."

"It's skinny and sad," Jasper said.

"Jasper is unhappy about the size of our family," Mom explained.

Jasper remembered scratching his back with the stick when it was an ordinary stick, before he had made it his Family Stick. "A small family is only good for scratching backs," he said.

"Scratching backs?" Dad said.

"Yes," Jasper said. "Can't we get a baby? Tomorrow I have to present my Family Stick at school. Do you see?" He pointed to the one purple leaf dangling from the stick. "I have a leaf all ready."

Dad said, "I am completely happy with the kid I

already have. I really, really don't want another baby."

Mom said, "A school presentation isn't a good enough reason to have a baby. Besides, having a baby takes a while. It's not something you do overnight."

Dad said, "Who wants dessert?" and Jasper knew he was changing the subject.

"I do," Mom said.

"I want a baby," Jasper said.

Then he got another idea, the best one so far. He was surprised he hadn't thought of it before.

After dessert, Jasper went over to Ori's house. He could hear the crying as soon as he climbed the fence to Ori's yard. Jasper knocked and waited a long time for someone to answer. While he was waiting, he remembered that he had told Ms. Tosh about seeing Ori's sister. He had told everybody the baby was purple. When they saw a purple baby, everybody would know she was Ori's sister, not his. He'd have to put a hat on her and bundle her up so not too much purple showed.

Finally, Ori's mother came to the door with dark circles like sunglasses around her eyes. She took the earplugs out and said, "Hello, Jasper."

"Can I borrow the baby?" Jasper asked.

"Borrow her?" Suddenly the sunglasses seemed to lift off Ori's mom's face. "Certainly! Of course you can! I'll go get her."

"I mean tomorrow," Jasper said, but Ori's mom was calling, "Ori! Come take the baby out with Jasper!"

"No!" Ori called.

"Jasper wants to," she said.

Ori came to the door wearing his earflaps hat,

followed by Ori's dad with the crying baby in his arms. Ori's dad was wearing dark circles around his eyes, too. "Would you like to hold her, Jasper?"

"Could I?" Jasper asked.

"Of course. You won't drop her?"

"No," Jasper promised.

Ori's dad showed Jasper how to support the baby's head so it wouldn't flop around. As soon as she was in Jasper's arms, she stopped crying and looked up at Jasper with her big, dark eyes. Ori's mouth fell open. "She stopped," he said. "She stopped." But when Ori's dad pulled the earplugs out of his ears and laughed, the crying started up again.

Ori's mother came back from the garage with the carriage. She took the crying baby from Jasper and placed her carefully inside, checking that the straps were done up properly. "Wa-wa-wa-wa!" the baby cried.

"Did you name her yet?" Jasper asked.

"That's her name," Ori told him. "Her name is Wa-wa-wa-wa."

Ori's mom told them to walk the baby up and down the sidewalk right in front of the house. Ori's dad went with them to the front yard and sat on a lawn chair to watch.

"Up and down," Ori's mother called. "I'll tell you when it's time to come in."

"Can I push her?" Jasper asked Ori.

Ori said, "Go ahead."

They walked up the sidewalk with Jasper pushing the carriage, then turned and walked back down. Ori dragged his feet and yawned, but Jasper felt proud.

"Do you think?" he asked.

"What?"

"Could I bring her to school tomorrow and pretend she's mine?"

"If you're asking me," Ori said, "sure. The thing is, my mom won't let you."

Jasper shrugged. "Everybody would know she's yours anyway. She's purple. I'd have to paint her or something."

It was too bad he couldn't borrow her, but at least the people who drove by might think that the baby was in his family. They might think he was the brother and Ori the friend. The only thing that spoiled the proud feeling of pushing the baby in the carriage up and down the sidewalk in front of the house was that the baby was crying so loudly.

Jasper told Ori about the dream he'd had the night before. "I came to school in my pajamas. The door was locked. I couldn't get in."

Ori said, "I think I remember what dreaming is. Yes. I remember sleeping, too."

"Does she ever stop crying?" Jasper asked.

"The thing is, no."

After they had walked up and down the sidewalk for a long, noisy time, Jasper started to feel bored. The boys wheeled the baby back into the yard. Ori's dad was slumped in the lawn chair snoring into his chest so Ori and Jasper left the carriage beside him. "Wa-wa-wa-wa!" the baby cried, and Ori's dad started to stir. The boys went inside to find Ori's mom.

She was in the bedroom, in the bed, fast asleep.

That night Dad came into Jasper's room to kiss the Star good night. He sat on the bed and said, "How's being a Star so far?"

Jasper shrugged. He didn't want to talk about Show and Tell. He especially didn't want Dad to know somebody had yucked at his belly-button lint.

"Everybody will like your Family Stick," Dad said.

"I wish it had more leaves," Jasper said.

"I know," Dad said.

"I wish it had more branches."

"I understand."

"I wish we had a bigger family," Jasper said. But he wasn't sure anymore that he wanted a baby to make it bigger. Not if they cried so much.

"Small families are good, too," Dad said.

"Big families are better," Jasper said. "They have bigger trees."

"Some of these big families?" Dad said. "The parents don't even know their own kids' names. Sometimes they move house and accidentally leave five or six kids behind."

Jasper said, "Name tags. And, at school? Ms. Tosh takes attendance every morning."

"You have an answer for everything, Jasper. I can see why you're the Star." Then he said, "Jasper, I've got an itch. Right between my shoulder blades."

Jasper sat up to scratch it. Dad moaned. "Ah! That's wonderful. Lower."

Jasper scratched lower. Then he scratched some letters and asked Dad if he could read them, which he could. He scratched H-I, and H-E-L-L-O and J-A-S-P-E-R. Dad asked Jasper if he needed a scratch, too, before he went to sleep.

"I think I do," Jasper said.

Dad scratched I L-O-V-E Y-O-U on Jasper's back, and it felt really good.

"Thanks," Jasper told him. Then he kissed Dad good night and lay down thinking that maybe, maybe, a small family wasn't so, so bad.

Chapter 5

At recess the next day, Isabel and Zoë got Ori and Jasper to play babies with them. They still had Halloween candy left over from last year, and they paid the boys with it. Isabel was Ori's mother, and Zoë was Jasper's mother. The boys lay on the grass and wailed while the girls went to collect food. Food was pinecones and twigs. As soon as Ori and Jasper finished pretending to eat the twigs and pinecones, they started wailing again for more food.

"You're not doing it loud enough," Ori told Jasper.

Jasper wa-wa-waed louder, so loudly that the

playground monitor came over to see what the problem was. She stared at where they were lying on the ground waving their arms and legs around.

"The thing is, we're pretending to be babies," Ori explained.

Jasper didn't say anything. Babies can't talk.

The playground monitor said, "Babies shouldn't be left alone. I'll stay until your mother gets back."

When the two mothers showed up a few minutes later with more food, the monitor asked to be paid for baby-sitting. Zoë gave her a pinecone. Jasper said, "We're doing it for Halloween candy. You should ask for that." The monitor laughed and moved on while the girls got down on their knees and hauled their babies onto their laps.

"Be careful of my star," Jasper told his mother.

"Eat up," Zoë said, waving a twig in Jasper's face.

"I want Halloween candy instead of twigs."

"I'm not giving it to you now. You'll just run off. You can have it when the bell rings," Zoë said.

"This is boring," Jasper said.

"I told you," Ori said. "Babies are boring. All they do is cry."

"Wa-wa-wa-wa!" Jasper cried. Then he decided to be a baby that bites. That was much more interesting, except before he'd even started biting, Zoë said to Isabel, "Maybe they're crying so much because their diapers need changing."

Jasper and Ori jumped to their feet. "No, we're not!"

Luckily, the bell rang just then, and the babies ran safely into the school. By the time they got back into the classroom, Jasper was having more second thoughts about getting a baby, even a pretty purple one. He'd forgotten about diapers! Who would change them? Mom and Dad made him clear the table. They made him make his bed. They would definitely make him learn to change diapers!

He had just slid into his place at his table when Ms. Tosh called on him to present his Family Stick. Jasper went over to his cubby and took it down. He carried it by the Styrofoam stand to the front of the classroom, and when he passed Zoë at her table, he whispered, "Where's my candy?"

Ms. Tosh said to everybody, "Kids, look. Jasper made a real tree." All the other Stars had made posters.

"It's a stick, not a tree," Leon said.

"That's right," Jasper said. "It's my Family Stick."

Everybody laughed, and Jasper felt pleased with himself.

"I see some leaves on your Family — Stick," Ms. Tosh said, smiling. "Tell the class about them."

"This leaf is me," Jasper said, pointing to his foil-covered leaf. "I made it in the shape of a star because I'm the Star of the Week."

"It looks like a Christmas decoration," somebody said, and Jasper felt extra pleased. He explained who the people were in the pictures glued to the green leaves.

"And what about that nice purple leaf?" Ms. Tosh asked. "Who is that?"

Jasper looked at the purple leaf. Because he was having second thoughts about getting a baby, he wished he'd taken it off. But he hadn't. There it was dangling from the stick. He thought about explaining how he had wanted to borrow Ori's sister, but he felt silly about that now. So he said the first thing that came into his head. He said, "That's my brother."

"Really?" Ms. Tosh said. "I didn't know you had a brother, Jasper."

"He doesn't," Ori said.

"I do," Jasper said, feeling his face heat up. "You just haven't met him. He doesn't go to our school."

"Oh, I see," Ms. Tosh said, like she really did understand. "What's his name?"

"Plum," Jasper said.

"Plum's not a name," Zoë said. "It's a fruit."

"It's not Plum then," Jasper said. "It's …" What? He thought of the man in blue coveralls who had come to the house to fix the oven the week before Jasper was the Star. There was a badge sewn over his pocket. The badge said *Earl*.

"Earl," Jasper said.

"Very interesting, Jasper," Ms. Tosh said in a different voice now, the voice she used when she didn't believe a word you were saying. "Thank you for sharing your Family Tree with us. You can go back to your seat now."

The Star of the Week set his Family Stick down on the Sharing Table where yesterday he had left the box of lint that nobody had understood either. He went back to his desk to start his work. Every time he looked up and saw the purple leaf hanging down from the stick, he felt sure he had a brother somewhere. Where? He had to find him. He had to find him or he'd be Liar of the Week.

Chapter 6

Being the Star of the Week was not going as well as Jasper John Dooley had expected. There hadn't been a banner draping the front of the school the first day. There hadn't been any kids chanting, "Jasper! Jasper! Jasper!" and waving little flags. Not even the kids in his class had chanted "Jasper!" Nobody had asked him the right questions during Show and Tell. Nobody had gone up to the Sharing Table to admire his Family Stick. Ms. Tosh hadn't even noticed that he hadn't gotten the lates once so far this week. By the end of the school day, when he turned in his star,

Jasper didn't dare ask Ms. Tosh if he was still going to be the Star tomorrow.

Mom met Ori and Jasper outside. "What's the matter with you boys?" she asked. "You look terrible."

Ori yawned. "Can I come over?"

Jasper said, "I'm still too busy."

"Did something happen today?" Mom asked.

"Yes," Ori said. "Jasper told everybody he had a brother."

"Jasper John. Did you say that?" Mom asked.

Jasper nodded.

"Why?"

"Because of the purple leaf on my Family Stick."

Mom looked worried, but just then Ori took his hat with the earflaps out of his backpack. He put it on his head and tied the strings in a bow under his chin. Mom laughed. "Why are you wearing a winter hat, Ori?"

"To protect my ears," Ori said, setting off down the alley.

"Am I still going to be the Star tomorrow?" Jasper asked as soon as Ori was too far away to hear.

"Of course," Mom said. "You're the Star of the Week."

"Ms. Tosh takes the star away every day. What if she doesn't give it back tomorrow?"

"Has that ever happened, Jasper? Has the Star of the Week ever been fired?"

"Not yet, but if I don't get myself a brother by tomorrow," Jasper said, "I'll be the first."

"Tomorrow?"

"Yes," Jasper said.

"And it has to be a boy?"

"That's what a brother is," Jasper said. "A boy."

As soon as they got home, Jasper went down to the basement where they had a workbench and some tools. Jasper liked to build things out of wood. He'd built an iceberg for his Nan when she went away on a cruise to Alaska. He'd made a soap dish for Mom. Now Jasper poked around in the big cardboard box of wood scraps. He found some long thin pieces he could saw into the right lengths. He had to be quiet sawing, though, and careful. Mom and Dad would be mad if he sawed himself.

A little while later, Jasper heard Dad come home from work and ask where he was. "In the basement," he heard Mom say.

Dad asked, "What's he doing down there?"

Mom said, "Getting the lint out of the dryer, I think." Then she said his dad's name in a very serious voice. "David? We need to talk."

"What is it, Gail?" his dad said, also very seriously.

After that Jasper could only hear whispering between his quiet sawing, and now and then a word. He heard, "Whisper, whisper, baby, whisper, whisper, whisper, maybe we should." They talked for a long time. Then Jasper heard his parents clomp down the basement stairs. They stood in the door holding hands and smiling big pretend smiles.

"Jasper John?" they said. "Could you stop for a minute? We'd like to talk to you."

Jasper quickly put down the saw. Mom and Dad didn't say anything about it. They just came over.

Mom said, "Jasper, if you're really unhappy —"

Dad said, "If the size of our family —"

"If you're disappointed in the way we are —," Mom said.

"What are you talking about?" Jasper asked.

Dad said, "Maybe we should talk about our too-small family."

"I'm too busy to talk now," Jasper told them. "I'm making myself a brother."

Chapter 7

It was a miracle that the Star didn't get the lates on Wednesday. He was up until ten o'clock the night before making his wooden brother Earl with Mom and Dad. When he woke the next morning, Earl's paint was dry, but Jasper had to rush to get to school on time. He put a pillowcase over Earl's head so that nobody would meet his brother on the way.

Jasper just made it, but Ori got the lates again. He staggered in while the class was doing the calendar. The Star of the Week, Jasper, slid the card that said *Wednesday* into the slot on the calendar. He slid in the month and the date. Then Ms. Tosh said, "Hurry, hurry, Ori."

Ori joined Isabel and Leon at his table. He looked really, really tired. He looked like nobody had made him brush his hair.

"Jasper," Ms. Tosh began. "Are you going to show the class what you've brought?"

"Yes," the Star answered. "I've brought my brother."

Everybody laughed.

"Your brother, Earl?" Ms. Tosh asked.

"Yes," Jasper said.

"Class? Would you like to meet Earl?"

"Yes!" all the kids cried.

"Presenting — Earl!" Jasper tore the pillowcase off his brother. Everybody laughed again. They fell into each other laughing. At first Jasper was hurt, but then he saw that Earl *was* funny looking. He had a purple face and long thin arms and legs and blocks of wood for feet. So many hands were waving in the air. Everybody had a question. They asked:

"Are you really allowed to saw?"

"Have you made other things out of wood?"

"Is making wooden people what you want to do when you grow up?"

Jasper answered all the questions. He felt proud. Ms. Tosh said she had a question, too. She asked, "Can you tell us, Jasper, how Earl is a Science Experiment?"

"A Science Experiment?" Jasper said.

"Yes."

"Is it Wednesday?" Jasper asked. He looked at the calendar and saw the word *Wednesday* that he had slid into the slot himself. "If it's Wednesday," he said, "then Earl is my Science Experiment."

Everybody got very quiet waiting to hear what the Star was going to say about his Science Experiment. Jasper waited to hear what the Star was going to say, too. He had no idea.

"Jasper?" Ms. Tosh asked.

"Earl is my brother. I named him after the man who came to fix our oven," Jasper began.

"He isn't really your brother," Isabel said. "He isn't real."

"That's my Science Experiment," Jasper said.

"How is that your Science Experiment?" Ms. Tosh asked.

"Shh," Jasper said, so he could think. He waited for some ideas. If he waited long enough, one or two usually came along. Finally, one did, just as a few kids were starting to squirm at their tables. Jasper asked, "Did you hear something?"

"No," they all said.

"That's because Earl didn't say anything. One of the ways you can tell that somebody isn't real is if they don't talk. Real kids talk all the time. They practically never shut up."

Even Ms. Tosh laughed when he said that.

"Now, put your hand here," Jasper said, placing his on his chest, right over the star. All the kids put their hands on their own chests.

"Do you feel something?"

"Yes!"

Jasper invited the class to feel Earl's chest. "Let me feel! Let me!" Everybody ran up to the front with reaching hands until Ms. Tosh made them stop pushing and line up properly. One by one everybody in Jasper's class got a chance to touch Earl.

"His body is a board," Ori said.

Ms. Tosh clapped her hands. "Okay, everybody. Back to your tables."

As soon as everybody was sitting down again, Ms. Tosh said, "Jasper has brought us an excellent Science Experiment. It teaches us one of the ways to tell if something is alive or not. Earl isn't alive. Why not?"

Everybody called out the answer: "He doesn't have a heart!"

Chapter 8

On Wednesday, Jasper didn't want to play babies with Isabel and Zoë, not even for Halloween candy. He didn't want his diapers changed. Also, he was too busy with his brother, poor heartless Earl. Ori didn't want to play babies either. He wanted to stay in the classroom and sleep in the Book Nook. Nobody ever stayed in the classroom during lunch unless they had gotten in trouble, but Ori said, "I don't care. I'm going to lie down in the Book Nook. Before you go to the lunchroom, cover me with pillows."

Jasper did. Then he and Earl ate lunch together in the lunchroom. Really, only Jasper ate. Earl stood beside him, leaning against the wall, grumbling because Dad hadn't packed Earl any lunch. Then Jasper and Earl went outside to play.

Isabel and Zoë came up to Jasper and Earl on the jungle gym. "Come on! Be babies!" they called.

"We're not babies!" Jasper said. "Babies are boring!"

"They are not!"

The girls kept bothering Jasper and Earl, who just wanted to climb in peace.

"You have to obey me!" Jasper called down to them. "I'm the Star of the Week!" He flashed his star at them.

The girls laughed at that, which made Earl so mad that he jumped down from the jungle gym and started to chase them away. Since he couldn't talk, he made growling sounds. Isabel and Zoë screamed.

"You better be careful!" Jasper shouted. "My brother doesn't have a heart!"

Zoë and Isabel were so terrified they ran right up to the monitor and told on Jasper. Terrifying other kids wasn't allowed at their school.

"It wasn't me!" Jasper said. "It was my brother!"

This was the strict monitor, not the nice one who would baby-sit for pinecones. She marched Jasper John and Earl straight to the principal's office.

"I can't go to the principal's office," Jasper cried. "I'm the Star of the Week!"

Mrs. Kinoshita was still eating her lunch in the staffroom. Jasper and Earl had to wait in the hall while the monitor went to fetch her. "Look what you did," Jasper told Earl. "Now I might lose my star."

A few minutes later, Mrs. Kinoshita showed up. She didn't seem very mad. She smiled when she saw Earl. Something green from her lunch was stuck in the smile, which made her seem even less scary. "Come in, boys," she said, pointing to the big chair across from her desk. Jasper had been in that chair before. It made him nervous because his feet didn't touch the ground. "Earl can't sit," he said. "His legs don't bend. Can I just stand with him?"

Mrs. Kinoshita let him. She asked, "So, Jasper John Dooley, what happened out there?"

The words rushed out of Jasper. "It wasn't me it was Earl the girls wanted us to be babies and he got mad. He doesn't know when he's being mean because he doesn't have a heart are you going to take away my star?"

Mrs. Kinoshita noticed the star then, shining on his chest. "Are you the Star of the Week, Jasper?"

Jasper nodded. He was surprised she didn't know. She was the principal.

Mrs. Kinoshita smiled, showing the friendly bit of green again. "Jasper, if you're the Star of the Week, nobody can take that away from you."

"Not even the principal?"

"Not even me."

Jasper felt much, much better then.

"So Earl is a bit of a troublemaker?" Mrs. Kinoshita asked, folding her hands on her desk.

"He's jealous," Jasper said. "He wants to be the Star, too, but I'm the Star this week."

"I understand," Mrs. Kinoshita said. "Did you know I once had two little boys?"

"What happened to them?" Jasper asked.

"They grew up. But when they were small? Oh, my goodness. They squabbled all the time. You used to be an only child, didn't you?"

"Yes."

"You must miss that now."

"I do!" Jasper cried. "If I was still an only child, I wouldn't be here in your office!"

Mrs. Kinoshita got up from her desk and opened her file cabinet. She rooted around for a minute. "That's funny. I don't have any record of Earl being registered at our school."

"He's not."

"Well, that's not allowed, Jasper. I'm afraid Earl can't go back to the classroom with you. I suggest he stay here with me for the rest of the day and you pick him up when it's time to go home. How does that sound?"

"Just a minute, Mrs. Kinoshita. Earl is saying something." Jasper leaned closer to his brother. He was starting to be able to understand Earl's grumbles and growls. "Earl says his legs hurt from standing all the time. Can he lie down in the sickroom?"

"Certainly. I'll take him over in a minute. You can go now, Jasper. The bell has already rung."

"Thank you, Mrs. Kinoshita," Jasper said. He whispered, "I don't think his legs really hurt. He just feels bad because he got in trouble."

Mrs. Kinoshita nodded. She knew how kids felt. "And congratulations on being the Star this week, Jasper," she said.

After he left the office, Jasper took his time

going back to his classroom, just in case math was happening there. He stopped to look at all the art on the walls. He drank from the water fountain. By the time he walked in the door, a big commotion was going on. It didn't seem to be about math.

Ms. Tosh asked, "Is Ori with you, Jasper?"

"No," Jasper said.

"Leon? Go get Mrs. Kinoshita. Hurry."

"I was just talking to Mrs. Kinoshita," Jasper said.

"I told her," Isabel said. "I told Ms. Tosh what you did with Earl."

Ms. Tosh didn't seem to care what Jasper and Earl had done. "Ori is missing," she said. "Nobody has seen him since lunch."

"He wasn't playing babies with us!" Zoë cried. "He said he would!"

"He didn't," Jasper said.

"He did, too!"

Jasper went over to the Book Nook and pulled all the pillows away. Ori sat up blinking. "You didn't want to play babies, did you?" Jasper asked.

Ms. Tosh put a hand over her heart. She said, "Oh, Jasper, you really are a Star."

After school, Jasper went to the sickroom to get Earl. He was lying on the cot with the blanket pulled up to his purple chin. "Wakie, wakie," Jasper told him.

They went outside to meet Mom and Ori. "Jasper!" Mom called. "I just found out from Ori that his mother had the baby! Why didn't you tell me?"

"I did. I said I wanted one, too. A purple one. But I don't anymore. I'm completely happy with the brother I already have. Well, not *completely*."

Ori said, "Jasper had to go to the principal's office today."

"Because of Earl," Jasper said. "Earl got me in trouble."

"Earl was bad," Ori said.

On the walk home, Jasper told Mom how Earl had terrified the girls and how he had to stay in the sickroom for the rest of the day. "He's not allowed back. He's not registered at our school," Jasper said.

"Oh, dear," Mom said. "It's not very nice to have to go to the principal's office during the week that you're the Star."

"Nobody can take my star away, Mom. Not even Mrs. Kinoshita. Even if I bring a Show and Tell that nobody understands. Even if I have a Family Stick instead of a Family Tree. Even if I forget to do a Science Experiment."

Mom stopped walking. "Jasper! We forgot the Science Experiment!"

"I'm still the Star."

Ori said, "Ms. Tosh said he really was one. *Really* a Star."

"I'm so sorry about your Science Experiment," Mom said. "I feel terrible."

"I feel great!" Jasper said. "I'm over the hump!"

"Over the hump" was something his Nan always said. It meant you had finished the hard part, and the easy part was coming up. The hard part about being the Star of the Week was the Show and Tell, the Family Tree and the Science Experiment. Sharing his Talent and Bringing a Special Snack for everybody to eat while they were writing Compliments to him — a piece of cake!

Ori asked Jasper, "You're not too busy today, are you? Can I please, please, please come over?"

"Sure!" Jasper said. "I'm over the hump!"

When they got in the house, Mom phoned Ori's mom to say he had come over to play and to congratulate her on the baby. Ori and Jasper went into Jasper's room. Jasper asked, "What do you want to do?"

Ori lay down on the bed and closed his eyes.

"I know," Jasper said. "Let's jump over some humps!"

Jasper gathered his stuffed toys and scattered them around the floor. He made Ori get off the bed so he could take the bedspread off and cover the stuffed animals with it. Under the bedspread they looked like humps.

"Okay," Jasper said, "let's start jumping."

He and Ori jumped. After a few minutes Ori asked if he could be a hump instead. He crawled under the bedspread and Jasper jumped over him. "You're the best hump!" Jasper told him.

When Jasper finally got tired of jumping over the humps, he went down to the basement to check the dryer screen. He came back up and read a book backward to see if the story turned out differently. Then it was suppertime.

"Well?" Dad asked when they were all sitting at the table. "What did they think of Earl?"

"They liked him a lot," Jasper said.

"Guess what?" Mom said. "Ori's mom had the baby. A little girl. She doesn't have a name yet."

"Yes, she does," Jasper said. "It's Wa-wa-wa-wa."

"Wonderful news," Dad said. "I'm glad it wasn't us!"

"And guess what else? We forgot Jasper's Science Experiment."

"Not so wonderful," Dad said.

"It was Earl's fault," Jasper said.

Mom got up from the table and went to the fridge to check the Star of the Week schedule. "Share Your Talent," she read.

"Jasper?" she asked, coming back to the table with a worried look on her face. "You'll have to be extra good at your Talent to make up for missing the Science Experiment."

"I will be. Don't worry."

The worried look didn't go away. She asked, "What talents did the other kids share?"

Jasper said, "Isabel did Scottish dancing. Leon played the violin. Ori played the violin. Paul C. played the violin."

"I wish we'd started you on the violin," Mom said. "I guess it's too late."

"Don't worry about my Talent," Jasper said.

"We're not very musical," Mom said.

"I'm musical," Jasper said. "I'm *really* musical."

"Really?" Mom said.

"Yes, you just worry about the Special Snack."

The phone rang and Dad got up to answer it. He said, "Congratulations! I just heard about the baby! Where's Ori? I don't know."

"Oh, no!" Jasper cried. "He's still a hump!"

Chapter 9

That night Jasper was very excited. Not only was he over the hump, he was going to have his first sleepover. His wooden brother Earl was going to sleep with him.

Mom and Dad stood in the doorway. "Don't talk all night," Dad said. "You have school tomorrow."

"You don't want to be too tired to Share Your Talent," Mom said.

Jasper said, "I won't."

"Are you sure about your Talent?" Mom asked.

"Yes," Jasper told her.

"Are you sure you're going to be comfortable tonight?"

"Please," Jasper said, "can you close the door? I'm ready for the sleepover to start."

Mom and Dad closed the door.

Jasper cozied up to Earl. Mom was right. It wasn't very comfortable sleeping with a person made of wood. It would be a lot more comfortable if Earl was wearing pajamas.

Jasper turned on the light. He got out of bed and went over to his pajama drawer, took a pair out and held them up for Earl to see. Earl didn't like them.

"They're nice," Jasper said. "They're my second favorite."

Earl let Jasper know that he wanted to wear the

ones with the sheep, the ones Jasper was wearing, Jasper's first favorite.

"Earl," Jasper sighed.

Jasper changed into the fire-truck pajamas. He dressed Earl in the sheep pajamas, then turned off the light and got back into bed. He felt sleepy. The night before, he'd been up way past his bedtime making Earl. He rolled over onto his side with his back to Earl. Earl jabbed him with his wooden arm.

"Stop it," Jasper said.

Earl didn't. He was a bit of a troublemaker. Jasper wiggled closer to the edge of the bed, out of Earl's reach. For a while, Earl lay there getting madder and madder because Jasper was falling asleep and not paying any attention to him. Jasper knew because Earl was making quiet little growling sounds that

Jasper ignored. Finally, Earl got so mad he leaned over and bit Jasper.

Jasper sat up with a howl. When Dad rushed in, Jasper hollered, "Earl bit me!"

There, sticking out of his shoulder, was one of Earl's teeth!

Dad pulled the sliver out, then said Earl wasn't allowed in Jasper's bed anymore. Earl had to sleep on the floor. Dad kissed Jasper good night for the second time and closed the door.

Earl lay all by himself on the hard cold floor. "It's your own fault," Jasper whispered down to him. "You ruined our sleepover. You have no heart."

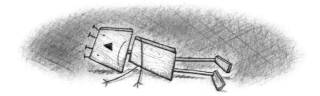

Chapter 10

The next day, both Jasper and Ori got the lates. Jasper really wanted to be on time because he knew Ms. Tosh would be waiting by her desk to take the star out of the drawer and pin it to his chest. The whole class would be waiting for him to do the calendar and Share His Talent. But two things happened. First, when Jasper got up — not late yet — he accidentally stepped on Earl, who was sleeping on the floor. Earl got really mad, and Jasper had to say sorry so, so, so many times. Then Jasper went into the kitchen where he found a book on the table next to Mom's coffee cup. The book was called *Name Your Baby.*

Jasper spent a lot of time finding a really good place to hide the book before Mom even realized he was up. "Jasper!" she called. "Jasper John!"

He came in from outside where he had been burying *Name Your Baby* in the garden. By then he had the lates.

Ori and Jasper ran into the school together. Jasper didn't want to be even later, but he had to tell Ori about the book. They stopped outside the classroom. "It's my own fault," he said. "I told her I wanted a baby. But now I don't. I changed my mind. What am I going to do?"

"Bring her over to our house," Ori said. "She'll change her mind, too, once she hears our baby."

Ms. Tosh poked her head out the door. "Boys? What's going on?"

"Nothing," Jasper said.

"We're waiting for you, Jasper."

Jasper and Ori went into the classroom. While Jasper got his star pinned on his chest, Ori went and sat at his table. Jasper noticed then that he looked really, really, really tired. He looked like nobody had told him to take off his pajama top and put on a shirt.

After they had done the calendar, Ms. Tosh brought a shoebox over from her desk. She asked the class to guess what was in it. Everybody shouted, "Lint!"

Ms. Tosh laughed. "No," she said, "but it has something to do with our Star. It has something to do with his Science Experiment."

The Star said, "There's a heart in the box," and everybody laughed, but he was right. Inside the box was a plastic model of a heart. It looked like a big purple fruit. Ms. Tosh let everybody hold it, then she showed them how it twisted open. Inside were four compartments, like in a jewelry box. Ms. Tosh explained how the heart sent the blood around the body. Jasper felt really sorry for Earl then. He didn't have a heart so he didn't have any nice warm blood squirting through his wooden body.

"Hey," somebody said, "look at Ori! He's wearing his pajamas!"

Ori looked down at himself. Everybody laughed and pointed. Ori was so embarrassed he turned as purple as his sister.

"The same thing happened to me!" Jasper said.

"Except I was wearing my bottoms, too! And no shoes! I came to school barefoot!" He started to tell the whole story about getting locked out of the school on the first day that he was the Star of the Week. Everybody forgot about Ori because they were laughing at Jasper's story instead. Jasper hadn't even got to the part about it being a dream when Ms. Tosh interrupted him.

"Jasper? I'm really looking forward to you Sharing Your Talent."

"Okay. May I please get a drink of water?"

Ms. Tosh let him go. She said, "Hurry, Jasper. We're all waiting."

Jasper hurried to the water fountain. He drank for a long time. He drank for so long Ms. Tosh stuck her head out the classroom door and said, "That's enough, Jasper." He marched into the classroom again, very confidently. He could hear the sloshing.

"What is Your Talent, Jasper?" Ms. Tosh asked when he was back standing in front of the class.

"Music. I'm going to play an instrument."

"What instrument are you going to play?"

"Me!" Jasper said.

Of course everybody laughed. They didn't believe him.

Jasper started very slowly, the way Ori had on his violin. He bent and straightened his knees. Faster, faster. He began to jump.

"He's jumping over the humps," Ori said.

"He's dancing," somebody else said.

"Listen," the Star said. "It's a song."

And then they heard it, the music coming from

Jasper, the sloshing of the water in his tummy. He was jumping so high now his heart was beating like a drum. His heart was playing, too.

"I hear it! I hear it!" everybody shouted.

And they all leapt up to play the song with Jasper. The song about being alive.

✶ ✶ ✶

On their way out of school at the end of the day, Jasper reminded Ori that they had a plan. Ori nodded. As soon as they met up with Mom outside, Jasper said, "Let's go over to Ori's. I want you to see the baby."

"We want you to hear her," Ori said.

Mom said, "What about the Special Snack?" She got an idea. "I know. Why don't we make extra and bring it over to Ori's? I really do want to see the baby."

Ori went home to tell his mom visitors were coming. Jasper and Mom went home to make the Special Snack. There was a little bag sitting on the kitchen counter when they got in. "That's a present for you, Jasper," Mom said.

Jasper reached in the bag and pulled out a cookie-cutter in the shape of a star. "Thank you!" he cried.

Mom powdered the counter with flour. She let the Star roll out the sugar-cookie dough. Sugar cookies were Jasper's favorite. He liked to lick the sugar sprinkles off the top after they were baked. Now he stood on a chair and drove over the dough with the rolling pin. "I'm flattening the hump," he said.

"How did Your Talent go?" Mom asked.

"It was great. I'll be the Star tomorrow for sure. But

what if nobody can think of any Compliments to write to me?"

"Did you write nice Compliments to the other Stars?"

"Yes," Jasper said.

"Then I'm sure they'll have nice things to say to you."

Jasper wished then that he'd written even nicer Compliments. He wished he'd *said* some Compliments out loud to the other Stars. Mom passed him the cookie-cutter. Jasper said, "I love this cookie-cutter. Look at how well it's cutting! What a great job it's doing making stars!"

"I'm glad you like it," Mom said.

"I love it!"

Mom laughed.

"I love you!" Jasper said.

"Oh, Jasper," Mom said. "That's so nice."

"I love Dad, too," Jasper said. "And Earl."

Jasper thought of a really nice thing to do for his poor wooden brother Earl, who scared people and bit them and had to sleep on the floor. He climbed off the chair and went to the drawer where all the kitchen things were jumbled together. After digging around for a bit, he found another cookie-cutter. It was in the shape of a heart.

"I'm going to make a special cookie for Earl," Jasper said. "Because I love him so much."

Too bad Earl couldn't write. Jasper would have got some really good Compliments for that!

As soon as the cookies were baked, the Star of the Week decorated four of them for Ori's family.

In icing, he wrote the nicest thing he could think
of — SHH! — then sprinkled all four with colored
sugar sprinkles. Jasper and Mom put the cookies
on a plate and carried them across the alley and one
house down.

They heard crying as soon as they were in the yard.
"Maybe this isn't a good time," Mom said.

"This is a really good time," Jasper said, ringing
the doorbell.

They had to ring twice. Ori answered wearing his
hat with earflaps.

"I don't think I told you before," Jasper said. "You
look nice in that hat, Ori."

"The thing is," Ori said, "it's really hot."

"I hear the baby," Mom said.

Ori pointed to the living room where the crying

was coming from. Mom went ahead with the cookies. Ori and Jasper smiled at each other behind her back because the crying was so loud. But when they got to the living room, Mom was giving the baby Compliments!

"Oh, isn't she darling! Isn't she sweet! I'd love to hold her!"

"Please do," Ori's mom said. As soon as Jasper's mom took the baby, Ori's mom stretched out on the couch. "Excuse me," she said. "It's been a hard week. Ori's grandmother was supposed to come and help, but she got sick. My sister is coming on Saturday, thank goodness."

"You're almost over the hump," Jasper told her.

"Yes, but poor Ori. He hasn't been getting much attention."

"I haven't been getting much sleep!" Ori said.

Jasper's mom was walking around the circle in the carpet with the baby, who still wouldn't stop crying. She was smiling at the baby, but she looked up to say, "Why doesn't Ori sleep over at our house tonight?"

"Please!" Ori cried over the crying. "Can I? Please?"

"I had a sleepover with Earl last night," Jasper said. "I'd like to try again."

Ori's mom said yes, and Jasper was so happy he almost forgot that they were there to show Mom how loud and boring babies were. And he almost forgot to say some Compliments. He told Ori's mom, "I like your new, smaller watermelon."

"Do you want to hold the baby?" Mom asked Jasper.

He did want to. Babies were loud, but they were only boring if you had to be around one all the time. If you just visited them, you saw they had tiny little hands that would curl around your finger and that they made googly faces in between their wails.

Mom passed him Ori's sister. "Hold her head like this."

"I know," Jasper said as he took her in his arms. Right away, the baby stopped crying and gazed up at Jasper with her big eyes. After a minute, her face didn't look so purple.

Ori undid the ties on his hat and pulled it off. Ori's mom sat up. Everybody Looked and Listened. Everybody smiled.

"How did you do that?" Ori's mom whispered.

"I'm the Star of the Week," Jasper said.

Chapter 11

Ori came for the sleepover right after supper. Jasper answered the door. "Did you bring your own pajamas?"

"I'm already wearing them," Ori said.

"Come in," Jasper said. "We're decorating the Special Snack for everybody to eat while they're writing Compliments to me. You can help."

Ori sat at the table with Jasper and Mom and Dad, his head propped up in his hands. He watched them draw the letter *J*, for Jasper, with icing then dip each

cookie in a bowl of sugar sprinkles, but he didn't
help. He said he was too tired. After all the cookies
were decorated, Ori said he was too tired to jump
over humps. He was too tired to play cards.

"I guess it's time to get ready for bed," Dad said.

"I'm already ready," Ori said.

"Go ahead," Dad said. "Jasper will meet you in bed."

Jasper changed into his sheep pajamas. He
brushed his teeth and washed his face. After he
said good night to his parents, he went to his room
where Ori was sleeping with the light on. Jasper got
quietly into bed. He leaned over the side to say
good night to Earl. "Uh-oh," Jasper said, "what's
the matter?"

He knew what the matter was. Earl was jealous.

"You would be sleeping here if you hadn't bit me," Jasper told him.

Earl looked mad. He was very, very purple.

"Listen, Earl," Jasper whispered. "If you're good tonight, I'm going to give you a Special Snack tomorrow. It's a Special Snack only for you."

Earl agreed and Jasper got up again to turn out the light. When he climbed back in the bed, Ori woke. "It's not morning yet, is it?" he asked.

"No," Jasper said.

"It's so quiet here," Ori said.

"That's because we don't have a baby."

"Not yet," Ori said. "Your mom really liked her."

Jasper said, "The book is still in the garden. She can't have a baby if she doesn't have a name for it."

"Yes, she can," Ori said. "My sister doesn't have a name yet."

"I thought you named her Wa-wa-wa-wa."

"That's just until we think of something better."

And then Jasper understood. Mom had set the book out to give to *Ori's* mom. He told Ori, "We have to make sure *your* mom never gets that book. There were hundreds and hundreds of names in it."

"Really?" Ori said.

"What if she finds a bunch of names she likes? What if she wants more babies just to use up the names?"

"Oh, no," Ori said.

"Some of these big families?" Jasper said. "The parents don't even know who their own kids are. Sometimes they move house and accidentally leave five or six of them behind. My dad told me."

"Oh, no!" Ori said.

"And what if you get an itch in the middle of your back? Who's going to scratch it?"

"The thing is, I don't know!" Ori started to cry.

Jasper didn't want another ruined sleepover. And he didn't want his friend to be sad. He patted Ori's shoulder and said, "Don't worry, Ori. I'm just across the alley and one house down. I'll come right over."

Ori sniffed a few times and said, "Thank you, Jasper," before he fell asleep again.

※ ※ ※

In the middle of the night, Ori climbed over Jasper and woke him up.

"Ow," Jasper said.

He thought Ori was getting up to use the bathroom, but Ori kept walking, so Jasper got out of bed, too, careful not to step on Earl sleeping on the floor. He followed Ori down the hall.

"It's back here," Jasper whispered when he caught up to Ori in the living room. Ori had stopped. He was standing in the dark, in his pajamas, staring at nothing.

"Do you have to go to the bathroom?" Jasper asked.

Ori shook his head.

"Come back to bed," Jasper said.

"Mom?" Ori said.

"Your mom's across the alley and one house down. We're having a sleepover. Remember?"

"Dad!" Ori called.

"Your dad's with your mom," Jasper said.

"Wa-wa-wa-wa?" Ori called.

"Her, too," Jasper said.

Dad came into the living room with his hair sticking up all over his head. He asked what was going on. Ori turned and walked right past them and out of the room. "Mom?" he called.

"He's sleepwalking," Dad told Jasper.

"Really?" Jasper said. "He's asleep?"

"Yes," Dad said.

"He's walking around asleep?"

"Yes."

"I want to!" Jasper cried. "How? How?"

"Shh. We shouldn't wake him," Dad said. "Let's see if we can get him back into bed."

Ori wandered into the kitchen. He seemed to be looking for something. Dad came up beside him. "Back to bed, Ori. This way."

"Is he dreaming us?" Jasper asked.

"We're probably in his dream all right," Dad said as he tried to shepherd Ori in the right direction. Ori scooted past Dad and found the back door. "Wa-wa-wa-wa?" he called. "Wa-wa-wa-wa?"

"He wants to go home," Jasper said.

"Let's take him home then," Dad said, opening the door and stepping out.

The moon was so bright Jasper and Dad had no trouble seeing where they were going. Ori seemed to be seeing with his feet. He went down the back stairs and started across the yard with Dad and Jasper following. The neighborhood was so quiet.

All the houses were dark. Only the owls and raccoons were awake. They were probably watching them and wondering what those crazy humans were doing.

"Is it the middle of the night?" Jasper asked.

"It is."

"We're walking around outside in our pajamas?" Jasper asked. "In the middle of the night?"

"Yes."

"In our bare feet?"

"Yes," Dad said.

Jasper said, "This is so, so, so much fun!"

As soon as they reached the alley, they could hear the crying coming from Ori's house. The kitchen light was on. "I guess they're awake," Dad said.

Ori crossed the alley. He walked alongside the fence

until he came to his own gate. Dad opened it and went ahead to explain why Ori was coming home.

"Wa-wa-wa-wa!" cried the baby from inside. Ori heard it in his dream, Jasper knew, because he smiled.

Then Jasper and Dad went back home. As soon as they were in the house, Jasper closed his eyes and started walking back to bed, making loud snoring sounds and trying not to laugh. Bonk! He bumped into the wall! Dad took him by the shoulders and steered him in the right direction.

"Zzzz," went Jasper. "Zzzzz."

All the way to his room, he kept his eyes closed with Dad guiding him. Then, when they reached Jasper's bedroom, Dad lifted Jasper and Jasper started to fly. Up in the air he sailed. He was sleepflying!

He landed back in bed, and when he fell asleep, he flew to other places he couldn't remember in the morning. All he remembered was the feeling of whooshing through the air. In his pajamas! In the middle of the night!

Chapter 12

The next day at school, Jasper handed out his Special
Snack to all the kids in his class. Everybody got a star-
shaped cookie with a sprinkly *J* written on it. While
they were eating their cookies and writing
Compliments to Jasper, the Star of the Week was
allowed to do anything he wanted. He could read a
book or draw a picture or play with Hammy, the little
brown hamster in the cage at the back of the room.
Jasper didn't do any of those things. He went over to
the cubbies and smelled all the jackets and sweaters
hanging there. When he smelled the fabric softener

clean-clothes-start-of-a-new-day smell that he loved, he checked the pockets for lint.

"Jasper John," Ms. Tosh called, "don't go snooping through other people's coat pockets."

"You said the Star could do anything he wanted."

"Snooping isn't nice."

"I'm not snooping," he said. "I'm looking for lint."

Ms. Tosh sighed and said, "Okay, just this once." Because he was the Star.

But not for much longer. At the end of the day, he had to turn in his star for the last time. When Ms. Tosh unpinned it from his shirt and shut it in the top drawer of her desk, Jasper thought he was going to cry. But then Ms. Tosh gave him another star, a paper one, but exactly the same size. "Jasper," she said, "you can wear this at home any time you want."

"I can still be the Star?" Jasper asked.

"When you try your hardest, when you're kind, then you're a Star."

"Really?" Jasper said. "How about when you're funny?"

"Sure," Ms. Tosh said. "When you make people laugh, you're being nice."

"You're a Star when you have a heart," Jasper said.

"That's it, Jasper," Ms. Tosh said. "That's exactly right."

She presented him with his Compliments Book. It had a nice construction paper cover with *Jasper's Compliments* written on it. Jasper hesitated before he took it. "What if somebody wrote a mean thing?" he asked.

"Nobody ever has," Ms. Tosh said. "I doubt they'd start with you."

Mom and Ori were waiting for Jasper outside the school. Jasper ran to them waving his Compliments Book. "Here it is!"

"What does it say?" Mom asked. "Can I read it?"

"Not yet," Jasper told her. "I'm saving it for later."

Ori said, "I left something out. I forgot to say sorry for ruining the sleepover last night."

"Ruining the sleepover?" Jasper said. "That was the best sleepover I ever had!"

First thing when they got home, Jasper dug *Name Your Baby* out of the garden and brought it to Mom. "There it is!" she said. "Where did you find it? And why is it full of dirt?"

Jasper told her what he'd done. "I hid it. But I'm the Star, and I have a heart, so I'm giving it back."

"Why did you bury it?" Mom asked.

"I was afraid you were going to get a baby. But I'm completely happy with our family the way it is."

"So am I," Mom said, and she gave him a hug.

"Well, not *completely*," Jasper said. "Earl is bossy. And —"

"What?"

Jasper blurted it out. "I like that baby so much!"

Mom nodded. "Me, too! She's so sweet and tiny and purple! You were right. She looks just like a plum."

Jasper said, "If only she didn't cry all, all, all the time!"

"I wouldn't want to listen to it," Mom agreed.

"If only she didn't have to wear diapers!"

Both of them yucked.

"But Mom?" Jasper said. "We can go over there any time we want, you know."

"You're right, Jasper. She's just across the alley and one house down."

"Maybe we can borrow her sometimes."

Mom laughed. "And when she starts to cry, we'll take her back."

"And when she needs a clean diaper?" Jasper said.

"Back she goes!" they cried.

✵ ✵ ✵

That night almost all of Jasper's not-too-small family ate supper together in the backyard. Jasper, Mom and Dad were there, and Jasper's Nan, who lived in an apartment nearby and wanted to hear everything that had happened during the week that Jasper was the Star and how he got over the hump. They even set a place for Earl.

"Who wants dessert?" Mom asked.

"Not me!" Jasper cried.

"No dessert?" Nan said, putting a hand on his forehead. "Somebody call nine-one-one."

"My Compliments are dessert," Jasper told her.

"Well, read them to us then."

"Yes," Dad said, "let's hear them."

All their hands were reaching for the book, and Ms. Tosh wasn't there to shoo them off. Mom had to do it. She said, "You read them first, Jasper. They're your Compliments."

Jasper lifted the book off his heart and opened it. Each page had a picture of Jasper and a Compliment.

He read:

Your orijinal!

I was so embarased when I came to school in my pajamas. But you saved me! !!!!!!! Your'e my brother. You never go WAWAWAWA!!!!.

Im colecting lint now to.

My dad says hes going to bild me a wodden brother.

You make me laugh, Jasper.

Good cokies. Did you make them?

I wish you really were my baby Jasper.

He knew Ms. Tosh's writing. She wrote:

Dear Jasper,

Never stop shining your light around.

Jasper looked up. The whole sky was twinkling at him. He closed his eyes and tried his best to shine back. When he opened his eyes again, he saw his nice small family around the table watching him read his Compliments, and he shone at them, too. Then Jasper turned the page and read the last Compliment.

I love you, Jasper.

"I love you?" He made a face. Yuck! "Who wrote *that*?"

Caroline Adderson lives in Vancouver, British Columbia, with her husband, her dog and the son who lied to them when he said he'd always be seven.

Illustrator Ben Clanton lives in Andover, Massachusetts, with his wife and puppy. Most days he doodles, and he always likes a good book. Ben is also the author and illustrator of *Vote for Me!*